Copyright © 2008 by NordSüd Verlag AG, Zürich, Switzerland.
First published in Switzerland under the title *Ich bin ein Wolf*.
English translation copyright © 2008 by North-South Books Inc., New York.

All rights reserved. No part of this book may be reproduced or utilized in any form or by any means,
electronic or mechanical, including photocopying, recording, or any information storage and retrieval system,
without permission in writing from the publisher.

First published in the United States, Great Britain, Canada, Australia, and New Zealand in 2008
by North-South Books Inc., an imprint of NordSüd Verlag AG, Zürich, Switzerland.
Distributed in the United States by North-South Books Inc., New York.

Library of Congress Cataloging-in-Publication Data is available.
A CIP catalog record for this book is available from The British Library.
ISBN 978-0-7358-2210-8 (trade edition)
Printed in Belgium
10 9 8 7 6 5 4 3 2 1

www.northsouth.com

GOOD LITTLE

WOLF

Kristina Andres

NorthSouth

NEW YORK / LONDON

I am a Good Little Wolf. Everyone says so.

In winter I keep all my friends cozy.

Sometimes I tell them I'll grow and GROW and GROW right through the roof!

But no one believes me.

I am a Clean Little Wolf.

I like to drip-dry with my friends.

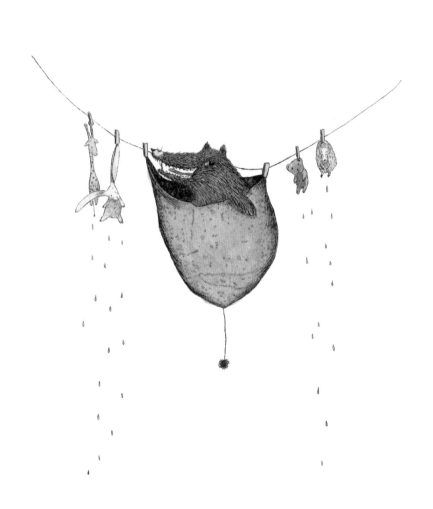

I am very helpful.

"Come in out of the rain," I tell everyone.

I sing them sweet lullabies about sailing over the moon.

And I tell them wonderful bedtime stories.

Once I even dressed up
like Little Red Riding Hood.

Sometimes I pretend I am a Big Bad Wolf!

But it's only just pretend.
Everybody knows
I am a Good Little Wolf.

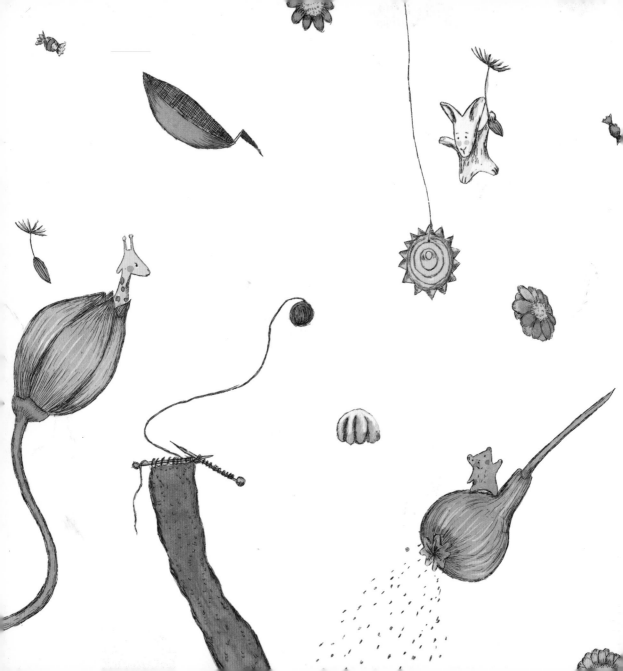